Photo Fame

Follow the Glitter Girls' latest adventures!
Collect the other fantastic books in the series:

1 Glitter FM
2 Magical Makeovers
3 Disco Divas
4 Ballet Babes
5 Party Poppers
6 Screen Stars
7 Fashion Show Fun
8 Spooky Sleepover
9 Christmas Crackers
10 Painting Party
11 Magazine Mania
12 Photo Fame

Look out for the Glitter Girls summer special!

Sunshine Superstars

Caroline Plaisted

Photo Fame

SCHOLASTIC

Scholastic Children's Books,
Commonwealth House, 1-19 New Oxford Street,
London WC1A 1NU, UK
a division of Scholastic Ltd

London ~ New York ~ Toronto ~ Sydney ~ Auckland
Mexico City ~ New Delhi ~ Hong Kong

Published in the UK by Scholastic Ltd, 2003

ISBN 0 439 98177 8

Typeset by Falcon Oast Graphic Art Ltd
Printed and bound in Great Britain by
Cox & Wyman Ltd, Reading, Berkshire

2 4 6 8 10 9 7 5 3 1

Chapter 1

It was a gloriously sunny afternoon and the Glitter Girls were making the most of the sunshine by having a picnic on the recreation ground after school.

"Who wants a sandwich?" Mrs Fisher, Charly's mum, asked.

"Yes, please," Hannah replied enthusiastically, looking up from the magazine she was reading. "There's a thing in here about customizing your school bags," said Hannah. "Look – aren't these ideas great?"

She held up the magazine for all her friends to see.

"That denim one is the best," said Mrs Fisher. "I'm surprised you Glitter Girls haven't thought about making your own bags before. After all, you've got your special jackets."

"We should!" said Meg. "We could do them at the weekend – what do we need to get to make them?"

Hannah quickly glanced at the magazine. "Well . . . you can use what you like really," she explained. "Badges . . . beads . . . hair slides . . . sequins . . . bits of ribbon . . . you just sew them on to your bag. You don't have to go out and buy special things."

"I know!" Flo exclaimed. "Why don't we copy the Glitter Girl writing on our jackets and see if we can adapt it for our school bags?"

"That's a cool idea," agreed Charly. "Do you think your mum would be able to help us with it, Hannah?"

"I'll ask her tonight," Hannah said. "And I'll take this magazine home with me and show it to her."

"Great!" said Meg, closing her notebook and

going back to looking at her own magazine.

"Oh, look – how cute!" Zoe pointed to a photograph in her magazine of a basket full of puppies.

"Oh!" sighed Charly. "They're gorgeous."

"There're some kittens too," said Zoe, turning the page.

"You've gone quiet, Flo," said Meg. "What are you reading about?"

"Oh," Flo looked up from her magazine. "It's an article about a veterinary hospital – you should read this, Zoe."

Flo handed the magazine to her friend.

"Thanks," said Zoe. "Here – swop you."

For the next few minutes, the Glitter Girls lay on the grass in silence, basking in the warmth of the autumn sunshine and engrossed in reading.

Suddenly Charly sat up and exclaimed, "Listen to this!"

The others sat up attentively.

"OK." Charly began reading from the magazine on her lap. "'*Girls Only! Ice Brite, the best-selling children's toothpaste, is looking for the Smile That's Right, The Smile That's Ice Brite to launch a new advertising campaign for Ice Brite Glitter, a FAB new glittery toothpaste, just for girls! If you think your smile can dazzle, why not go along to the Ice Brite audition in Birmingham?*' Look!"

"Wouldn't it be cool to be the Ice Brite Smile?" Zoe said, not realizing the joke that she'd made until Charly, Flo, Hannah and Meg giggled.

"How old do you have to be?" Hannah asked.

"Erm. . ." Charly read some more. "You just have to be over five."

"Can I see?" Meg asked.

Charly handed it over and pointed to the bottom of the page. "The article's just here."

"I can't wait to see what glittery Ice Brite looks like!" exclaimed Hannah.

"So what do you have to do at the audition?" Flo wondered.

Meg looked up from Charly's magazine. "It says you can sing and dance, or read something, like a poem."

"I'd love to be the *Smile That's Right*," said Charly.

"Wouldn't we all?" said Zoe, smiling her best Brite Smile.

"Precisely!" confirmed Meg, grinning at her four best friends.

Charly, Zoe, Flo and Hannah looked puzzled. Meg explained, "Well, I was just thinking how cool it would be to go along to the audition."

"But didn't you say it's in Birmingham?" said Mrs Fisher. "That's a long way to go, girls."

"Oh!" said Charly. "Mum! Please!"

"When is the audition?" Zoe asked.

"Hmm. . ." Meg read through the details. "The 18th."

"But that's next weekend!" said Flo.

"We've got to go!" said Charly. "Please Mum! Can we?"

Mrs Fisher looked at her daughter and smiled. "Well . . . I don't know, Charly."

"But Mum, it would be so much fun!" Charly pleaded.

"Yes," agreed Zoe and Hannah.

"Girls," Mrs Fisher said. "I know it would be fun, but don't forget that there will be hundreds of other children at the audition. And some of them will probably be professional models."

"But if they only wanted professionals they wouldn't be advertising in a magazine, would they?" Meg suggested.

"Maybe not," Mrs Fisher agreed. "But it's not up to me to decide if you can all go, is it? I can only make a decision for Charly."

Charly looked pleadingly at her mum.

"Can I go," she begged. "Please?"

Mrs Fisher looked at her daughter's eager

face and those of her four friends. Finally, she said, "OK Charly – if everyone else's mums and dads agree, I'll let you go."

"Yes!" Charly punched the air with excitement.

"But only if everyone else is going," Mrs Fisher warned.

"Well we'd better ask them all tonight!" said Meg, grinning.

"Go Glitter!" her friends agreed.

Chapter 2

As soon as they got home, the Glitter Girls started to ask their parents if they could audition.

Flo was the first to telephone everyone and tell them that her dad had said yes!

"I told him that Charly was going and that it was for toothpaste!" Flo explained to each of her friends in turn. "He said every dentist's daughter should advertise toothpaste – so I can go!"

"My mum has said I can go if everyone else can," said Hannah when she rang round. "So you lot are going to have to persuade your parents too!"

"Oh my mum went on for ages saying how

many hundreds of girls will go to the audition and tried to put me off," Zoe had told the other Glitter Girls when she rang them. "But I told her how much we all wanted to go and just have fun – so she's said yes!"

Meg had her friends worried because she was the last one to ring them all up and she sounded a bit fed up when she eventually called.

"Huh!" Meg said. "My mum won't talk any more about it until she's called everyone else's parents! It's so not fair!"

"Don't worry," Charly had comforted Meg. "If everyone else has said yes, she's bound to agree!"

By the end of that evening, every one of the Glitter Girls' mums and dads had spoken to each other. All the Glitter Girls were allowed to go! After checking the magazine again, they discovered that the audition was going to be at the National Exhibition Centre, so it was agreed that Mr Gordon, and Meg's and Flo's mums would go with the girls by train to Birmingham. The Glitter Girls' next adventure had begun!

★ ♥ ★ ♥ ★ ♥ ★

The Glitter Girls huddled excitedly in the play-ground at break the next day.

"I can't believe that we're going to be auditioning for Ice Brite!" Charly grinned, hardly able to contain her excitement.

"It's going to be fantastic," said Zoe. "What do you think glittery toothpaste looks like?"

"Cool!" said Hannah.

"What do you think the audition will be like?" Flo wondered.

"Perhaps a bit like the talent competition," suggested Meg.

"My mum reckons there will be hundreds of girls there – maybe even some professional child models and actors," Hannah said. "She thinks that we'd have to do something really amazing to make ourselves stand out from the rest."

"But if we have our Glitter Girl jackets on we'll certainly stand out, won't we?" Flo said.

"I definitely think we should wear them," agreed Meg.

"What should we do at the audition?" Charly asked.

"Maybe we could make up a dance!" exclaimed Hannah.

"Good idea," Zoe agreed. "And we could sing too!"

"But have we got to audition on our own?" asked Flo. "I'm not sure I want to do that."

"It didn't say anything about that in the article," Meg remarked.

"Aren't they only looking for one girl though?" said Hannah.

"I thought this was for all of us!" exclaimed Zoe. "We can't audition against each other!"

The Glitter Girls did everything together and

didn't want to be in competition with any of their best friends.

"Zoe's right," said Charly. "We want to do this together!"

The Glitter Girls looked at each other anxiously. It was Flo who came up with a solution.

"Tell you what," she said. "We don't know how many girls they are looking for, do we? So why don't we just work out some kind of song and dance routine that we all do together? That way we can show them how good we all are!"

"That sounds cool," said Hannah. "And I could always work out a routine where each of us gets to do a bit of a solo. . ."

"What – like S Club Juniors?" Charly wondered.

"Exactly!" said Hannah.

"Go Glitter!" her friends cried in agreement.

The Glitter Girls met up after school that afternoon to work out their audition piece.

"We haven't got long until the 18th," Meg explained. "So we need to get our routine sorted straight away."

"Well, I've been thinking," said Charly, pushing her glasses back up on her nose. "If we want to stand out from the crowd we should use the words that they mention in the magazine!"

"Good idea," said Zoe. "The smile that's right – the smile that's Ice Brite!"

"But I'm hopeless at writing rhymes," Hannah moaned.

"Let's think," said Meg, opening her notebook. "First we need a catchy tune that everyone knows. If we've got the tune, then the words might come more easily."

"OK," agreed Hannah. "Let's think of our favourite hits."

After a few minutes, the Glitter Girls all

agreed that one of their favourite tunes to dance to was Geri's "It's Raining Men" – they'd all danced to it at the last school disco. Without thinking, they all started to hum the tune.

"Hey," said Meg after a while. "How about this?"

She started to sing to the tune.

"We've got great smiles! (Shiny white!)
We've got great smiles! (Ice Brite!)
Shiny! White! Ice Brite Right!
Glittery smiles that shine Ice Brite!"

"Yes!" said Charly and she started to sing along with Meg. The others joined in enthusiastically.

"How about moving like this?" Hannah suggested, putting some dance steps together that the others copied.

"Hey, this is good!" said Meg when they took a breather. The others agreed.

"Do you think we'll stand out?" Zoe asked.

"If we wear our glittery clothes we should!" said Hannah.

"Should we have any props? You know, maybe banners that say Ice Brite or something!" Charly suggested.

"I know!" said Flo. "We could make a tube of Ice Brite!"

"Then we could use it in our routine!" Hannah agreed enthusiastically.

"Sounds great to me," said Meg. "But do you think you could make one?"

"If my sister can help me," said Flo.

"Go Glitter!" they all cheered at once.

Chapter 3

With just a few days before the audition, the Glitter Girls had to work hard to make sure that their song and dance routine was as eye-catching and perfect as it could be. But first they had to learn it! Because they already knew the tune though, it didn't take that long – and they made a recording of "It's Raining Men" from a karaoke CD that Kim, Flo's sister, had. There was no vocal on the CD so the Glitter Girls could sing their own words over the music.

When they weren't practising, the girls made a giant tube of toothpaste out of cardboard. Kim helped them to make the basic shape and then they stencilled "Glitter Brite" on the tube and painted it glittery pink. Then they made a big pink toothbrush to go with it.

"They look fantastic!" said Charly when the toothbrush and toothpaste were finished and dry enough to touch.

"They won't be able to miss us with these, will they?" smiled Meg.

"I can't wait for us to rehearse using them," Hannah said.

The Glitter Girls had worked out their dance routine so that they all stood in a line behind the toothpaste at the beginning of the number. Charly held it at the front and then, as they started to each sing a line of their rhyme, they jumped out at alternate sides of the toothbrush. By the end of their routine, three of them were holding up the toothpaste and the other two the toothbrush. It was so cool!

Before the Glitter Girls knew it, it was Friday afternoon. The 17th. The night before the audition. They were gathered in Hannah's bedroom, checking through the things they needed to take with them to Birmingham the next day.

"OK," said Meg, running through the list she'd made in her notebook. "Are we all cool about what we're going to wear?"

Each of the Glitter Girls went through the list of pink, purple and glittery clothes that they had chosen to wear for the audition.

"So what else do we still have to do, Meg?" Zoe asked.

Meg looked back at her list. "Remember to take the backing track."

"I'll have that," said Charly.

"But we've also got to get the giant tooth-brush and toothpaste there, haven't we?" Hannah said.

"I've wrapped them up in some big bin bags," Flo explained. "We should be able to carry them between us somehow."

"Good – then no one else will see them till we're on stage!" Charly smiled and pushed her pink glasses back up on her nose. "We don't want any of the others at the audition to know what we're going to do, do we?"

The others murmured their agreement.

"We'll do our hair and make-up when we get there too," said Meg. "After all, we don't want it to get messed up when we change."

"Good idea," agreed Hannah, running her fingers through her fringe as she spoke. "I'll bring my ballet bag – it's got hairpins and hair-spray and stuff."

"Looks like we're all ready then," said Meg, closing her notebook.

"I can't wait until tomorrow!" Charly said, hugging her knees to her chest.

"Nor me," Zoe agreed as she plaited one section of her hair.

"So we meet at my house at seven thirty," Hannah confirmed.

The Glitter Girls looked at each other and grinned.

Flo looked at her watch. "I said I'd be home at six."

"Me too," Meg, Charly and Zoe said.

There was half an hour to go.

"What shall we do now then?" Zoe wondered.

"One more practice!" Charly suggested.

"Go Glitter!" her friends agreed and jumped up, ready to start.

Chapter 4

"Come on, you lot!" Mr Gordon called. "If we miss that train there'll be no point in going to Birmingham."

It was seven thirty and the Glitter Girls were all gathered at Hannah's house as arranged. They were feeling excited and nervous at the same time.

"Has everyone got their outfit?" Meg asked, checking against the list she had written in her notebook.

"Yes," her four best friends replied.

"Hannah – have you got your ballet bag with all the hair stuff?"

"Here it is!" Hannah grinned.

"And you don't have to ask if Flo's got the

props!" Zoe giggled, pointing to the huge bin bags that were sitting in the hallway. You could just see a bit of pink glitter poking out of one of them.

"I've got a picnic to keep us all going," Mrs Morgan said, pointing to a bag by the front door.

"Great!" said Charly.

"Come on then – let's get to the station!" said Mr Gordon.

"Have a fantastic time, girls!" Mrs Gordon kissed Hannah goodbye.

"And don't forget," warned Dr Baker, "that it's meant to be fun! It doesn't matter if they don't choose one of you."

"No," said Charly. But all the same, she really hoped that one of the Glitter Girls was going to be chosen as the Ice Brite Smile. And secretly, all her friends felt the same.

"I think we just follow the crowd," Mrs Eng suggested when they all stepped off the train a couple of hours later.

"There are loads of people here," Meg said, looking around the crowded train station.

"Do you think they're all here for the audition?" Flo wondered.

"Perhaps some of them have come to see the exhibition that's on here," Mrs Morgan said, realizing that the size of the crowd was making the Glitter Girls nervous.

"Hey, look!" Charly said. "There's a sign over there!"

Everyone looked over to where she was pointing. It read: ICE BRITE AUDITIONS THIS WAY!

"Most of the others seem to be going that way," Zoe said, looking around at lots of girls, similar in age to the Glitter Girls and all dressed in really great clothes.

"Do you think we stand a chance?" Flo asked.

"Maybe Mrs Gordon was right," suggested

Charly. "Maybe lots of them are professional models."

"Maybe," said Zoe. "So we won't stand a chance, will we?"

"Don't be silly!" Meg said, hugging her friend. "I mean – who else has got the props and the dance routine and the smiles that we have?"

Immediately the four other Glitter Girls felt better.

"She's right," Hannah said, breaking into a smile again.

"Let's show them what we can do!" agreed Flo.

"Go Glitter!" they all yelled.

"OK – I need your name and your age, please!"

The Glitter Girls were standing in a long queue, just inside the entrance to the exhibition hall. One by one, the Glitter Girls gave their names and ages to a girl called Miranda, who was scribbling things down on a clipboard and giving each of them a number. She was about to move on to the next person in the queue when Meg spoke up for her friends.

"Excuse me – can you tell us where we can change? There will be time, won't there?"

"No worries." Miranda smiled at them. "You can change in the cloakrooms over there. But make sure you are back here in half an hour! OK, good luck – next please!"

The girl behind the Glitter Girls moved forward in the queue.

"Come on," said Charly. "We've only got half an hour to make ourselves look great!"

★ ♥ ★ ♥ ★ ♥ ★

"Anyone else need any hairspray?" Mrs Morgan asked.

They were crowded into the small changing room amongst lots of other girls.

"Me, please," Charly put her hand up.

"Close your eyes then!" Mrs Morgan gently covered Charly's hair in a fine mist of the glittery spray.

"Don't you all just look fantastic!" said Mrs Eng, smiling at the five best friends.

It was true. The Glitter Girls looked at each other in the big mirror in the cloakroom and grinned at their reflections.

"Time's up!" said Zoe, looking at her pink flowery watch.

"Come on – we don't want to miss our chance!" exclaimed Meg.

"We'll be watching you from the audience," grinned Mrs Morgan.

"Good luck, girls," Mrs Eng smiled. "We'll take your bags but you'd better take your props."

"Thanks!" The Glitter Girls rushed out of the cloakroom, their arms full of their props, and bumped straight into Mr Gordon who was waiting patiently outside.

"Whoa! My goodness," he said. "I hardly recognized you! Come on, smile for the camera!"

"Go Glitter!" the five best friends all yelled at once.

Chapter 5

There was a big platform at one end of the hall and the panel of judges was seated right in front of it. Suddenly the enormous room fell silent as one of them stood up.

"Hello, everyone! I'm Matt and I'm the director of the two Ice Brite Glitter commercials that we are auditioning for today. I'd like to introduce you to Catriona who's from Ice Brite and who is here to help us to make sure we get the right smile today. . ." A lady with short dark hair stood up and smiled at everyone. Then Matt started to speak again. "We've also got Vicki here with us, who is going to choreograph the commercial." Matt pointed out another girl next to him. "There's lots of you to see today so we'd better get on with things. OK – Miranda, let's have the first girls on stage please!"

The audition had begun.

★ ♥ ★ ♥ ★ ♥ ★

For a large part of the audition, the Glitter Girls stood around with everyone else, not doing much at all. Eventually though, they got their chance to go up on the stage with a group of about twenty girls. The first thing they had to do was step forward, one at a time, to say their name and age again.

"Don't forget to smile!" Meg whispered as she went up with her friends.

But seconds later, their group was called off the stage again.

"What do you think they'll do next?" Flo whispered to her friends once they were sitting down again.

"Decide who gets a chance to do their audition piece, I expect," said Charly.

"You mean some people will have come all the way here just to say their name and age?" Zoe said, amazed.

"That's right," said Meg. "Isn't it awful?"

After about another hour, Miranda came back and explained that only some of them were being called back for the next session.

"Listen carefully," Miranda said. "If we don't call your number, thank you for coming along today but, we're sorry, you aren't through to the next round. If we do call you though, please stay in your seat."

The friends grabbed each other's hands and held them tight. Were any of them going to be asked to go home already? Each of them was still hoping that one of the Glitter Girls was going to be chosen as the Ice Brite Smile. At the same time they were dreading being one of the girls asked to leave. The butterflies in their tummies fluttered anxiously. But soon the girls' worries were over – all five of them had been called for the next round!

"Go Glitter!" they all said.

Miranda told them all to take their seats again and explained that they would be called up in turn to do their audition piece.

"Good job we decided to do a dance – seeing as one of the judges is a choreographer," Hannah whispered to her friends, and they all gave her a nervous smile of agreement.

★ ♥ ★ ♥ ★ ♥ ★

There was a lot more hanging around before the girls were called on stage. Or at least, when Zoe was called by Miranda.

When all five of them stood up at once, Miranda looked at them, puzzled. "Er, I only want one of you. . ." She looked down at her clipboard. "Which one of you is Zoe?"

"Oh – we're going to do our dance together," Hannah explained.

"Together?" the girl looked worried.

"Yes," said Zoe. "We're best friends, we do everything together."

"I see," she said. "I'll need to explain that to our panel of judges."

"They will let us do our piece together, won't they?" Meg asked. "We've rehearsed it that way so we have to!"

Miranda was still looking anxious. "Well it's not usual, I must say. I'll have to go and ask the judges if it's OK. Wait here a moment."

The Glitter Girls looked at each other.

"What will we do if they say no?" Zoe asked.

"We're best friends, aren't we?" Meg said, looking at her friends. "We do everything together – if they say no then we'll just have to leave now. Agreed?"

"Agreed!" the Glitter Girls said, crossing their fingers and hoping the judges would say yes.

It wasn't long before Miranda came back over to them.

"OK – they've said yes. Have you got any backing music?"

Zoe handed the tape to Miranda.

"You'll need to get over by the stage as soon as possible. Wait at the back of the queue."

"OK," nodded Flo.

"Phew!" said Meg. "Come on, let's get the wrapping off our props and go!"

The Glitter Girls, along with their toothbrush and toothpaste, joined the other girls by the stage.

One by one, the girls in front of them went up to perform their piece. Some of them sang, some danced, some recited poems. All of them were really talented.

"This is really scary!" whispered Flo. "Why are we doing this?"

"It'll be fine," said Hannah. But she didn't sound like she believed it.

"It's your turn now!" said Miranda, ushering them on to the stage. "Good luck!"

Meg, Flo, Hannah, Zoe and Charly looked at each other and gulped.

"Go Glitter!" they whispered.

★ ♥ ★ ♥ ★ ♥ ★

The Glitter Girls danced, sang and smiled, just as they had at home. Only this time they were under dazzling lights and in front of the crowd of girls, parents – and the panel of judges. It seemed like only a few seconds before their routine was over.

"Thank you, girls!" said Matt. "OK – next!"

Back in their seats, the Glitter Girls looked at each other.

"What do you think?" Zoe asked.

"Did we do OK?" Hannah wondered.

"I don't know," said Meg. "I think we did our best."

"Is this your first audition?" said the girl who was sitting next to Charly. She had shoulder-length dark hair and was smiling at the girls.

She seemed really friendly.

"Yes," said Meg, smiling back. "Is this your first too?"

"Oh no – I do lots," she explained. "I've done a couple of commercials on television already. I'm afraid no one ever tells you much at these things and you always have to wait around for ages. My name's Catherine, by the way."

"Hi, I'm Flo," said Flo grinning. "And this is Meg, Charly, Zoe and Hannah. Do you always have to audition with so many people?"

"No – this is way bigger than any other audition I've done. But I thought you were really cool. Everyone stopped to watch you!"

"Thanks," said Meg. "You were good too."

"Hey look – Miranda's coming over!" exclaimed Zoe.

"Now's our chance to find out which of us stays for the next round," said Catherine. "Good luck!"

Chapter 6

"OK," Miranda said, smiling around at them all. "We're really cutting down now. Thanks to everyone who came today and well done to the following – who we'd like to see again. . ."

There was total silence as numbers were called out.

"We've all made it!" Meg said, hugging her friends as all their numbers were called.

"And so has Catherine!" smiled Zoe.

Catherine winked at them as Miranda asked all of the girls staying to assemble in one corner of the hall.

"OK," Miranda said. "Well done for getting through. Now it's time for you to take a lunch break but we'll need you back in half an hour to do your audition pieces again. See you then!"

★ ♥ ★ ♥ ★ ♥ ★

It was a long day. After the Glitter Girls ate their picnic lunch with their parents, they checked their appearance in the cloakroom before going back to meet Miranda and the other children.

"I think I can count fifty of us," Meg said, looking round.

"Hey – there's Catherine!" said Zoe, pointing up to the stage.

The Glitter Girls, who had been told to sit in the seats a few rows behind the judges, gave her a thumbs up as she smiled and started to sing her song.

"She's good," Hannah whispered to her friends.

But it seemed that everyone who went up on stage was good! When it was the Glitter Girls' turn to do their piece again, they put every ounce of energy and talent into their performance. Eventually Miranda came over and told them they were down to the last eight. So was Catherine!

"This is great and awful at the same time!" sighed Charly.

"I know," agreed Flo. "I mean – what if all five of us are turned down now!"

"But what if only one of us gets to stay. . ." said Meg, looking anxious.

It was late in the afternoon when all of the finalists were asked to go up on stage again. This time, they weren't asked to perform anything – and the Glitter Girls weren't allowed to go up together either. They were filmed as Miranda asked them some questions – things like what were their favourite TV programmes and groups, who was their best friend and so on.

As they spoke, the video footage was being

played back on a huge television screen that the judges were looking at.

"OK," said Matt when they had finished. "Can you all give us a few minutes and then we'll announce our decision."

"I'm so nervous I think I'm going to be sick!" said Hannah.

"I can't believe we're down to the last eight!" said Zoe excitedly.

"I've done this lots of times," said Catherine. "But I still feel nervous at this bit."

After that, no one spoke much until the director came over to where they were sitting.

"Well, girls – thanks so much for coming along today." He looked around at the group and smiled. "You've had a long day and we're really impressed with your talent. We wish we could hire you all but we can't. It's been a truly difficult decision – in fact we've made a decision that none of us anticipated making. We've decided. . ."

The Glitter Girls looked at each other, their eyes wide with excitement and dread.

". . .that we're going to have five of you. You five girls, er, the Glitter Girls!"

"Go Glitter!" the five best friends screamed! "Yes!"

"Now, thanks to the other three of you who auditioned today. It's not because you're not talented, and we want to keep your details on file for other things. Please make sure Miranda's got your contact information before you go," said Matt, then he turned back to the Glitter Girls. "I'll just need to have a quick word with your parents."

"Well done," Catherine said, coming to say goodbye. "You deserve it."

"Thanks Catherine," said Hannah, giving her a hug.

"Good luck at your next audition," Flo said.

"It was really good to meet you," smiled Charly.

"And you," said Catherine. "Anyway, have fun making the Ice Brite commercial."

"Thanks – and bye," the Glitter Girls said.

"Well done, girls!" said Mr Gordon and Meg and Flo's mums as they rushed over to congratulate them.

"You must be the girls' parents," Matt smiled, shaking their hands. He explained that the commercials were going to be shot in Birmingham the next week, and that the girls would each receive a set amount of money as their fee for modelling. The Glitter Girls chattered away about what they might spend some of the money on, until Meg's mum said that they would have to wait and discuss all that with their parents.

"We'll need your daughters for two days filming and then one extra day for shooting still photography for a magazine campaign. We'll put you all up in a hotel – does that sound OK?" Matt asked.

A hotel? Two days making commercials and a day taking photographs? Was that OK?

"Go Glitter!" they all yelled.

Chapter 7

It was decided that Zoe's mum and Flo's dad would go with the Glitter Girls to Birmingham. On the Tuesday afternoon, after school, the Glitter Girls gathered at Zoe's house.

"Come on, girls," smiled Dr Baker. "I think we should catch that train, don't you?"

"Yes!" they all agreed.

"Have a great time, girls!" Mrs Fisher said, kissing Charly goodbye.

"Bye Mum – I'll miss you," said Charly.

"Be good!" smiled Mrs Gordon as she hugged Hannah.

"And don't stay up too late in that hotel!" Mrs Morgan said, pulling a serious face.

But everyone just giggled. The Glitter Girls

were off on another great adventure!

★ ♥ ★ ♥ ★ ♥ ★

By the time the Glitter Girls got to Birmingham that night, they were too tired to stay up very late. They were met by a girl called Scarlet from the production company that Matt worked for. She took them to a big hotel in the centre of Birmingham and the girls were thrilled to find that they had a huge suite of rooms to share. It meant that they were all sleeping in the same room and Dr Baker and Mr Eng had rooms on either side of them. There was a huge bathroom with a big round bath – it even had a television encased in the wall.

On Wednesday morning, the Glitter Girls couldn't believe it when Scarlet arrived with a chauffeur and a long limousine to take them to the studio where the commercials were going to be made.

"This is just so cool!" said Charly as she settled into the back of the car.

"Hey look, there's even carpet up the walls!" exclaimed Hannah.

The Glitter Girls sat back in luxury as they whizzed across Birmingham to the studio. The car was so big that Dr Baker and Mr Eng were in a separate section in front of the Glitter Girls!

Matt met them at the studio doors. Vicki, the choreographer who had been at the audition, was there too.

"Great to see you, girls! Come in," said Matt, ushering them into a big room with lots of comfy sofas.

"How are you all?" Vicki asked.

"Fine, thanks." Charly smiled.

"Good," said Matt, sitting down on one of the sofas. The Glitter Girls sat down with Zoe's mum and Flo's dad too. "We've got lots to do over the next three days if we're going to complete both the commercials as well as the still photography. You're going to be exhausted by the time you go home!"

The Glitter Girls grinned excitedly.

"So what happens first?" Meg asked.

"We're going to run through the story-boards," Matt explained.

"What are they?" Zoe asked.

"These things," said Scarlet, holding up some big pictures. "They explain the sequence that the commercial will take."

"Vicki's going to teach you two numbers," said Matt.

Vicki smiled at the Glitter Girls. "We'll learn them this morning."

"Cool," said Hannah.

"Right, let's go through the storyboards," said Matt.

He and Scarlet explained to the Glitter Girls that the theme of both commercials was about having fun and looking great.

"The commercial is going to be set in a winter scene with lots of snow and shimmer," Matt explained.

"And, of course, showing off your great Glitter smiles!" added Scarlet.

"Hey, that sounds great," said Meg.

"Really cool," agreed Zoe.

"Well," Scarlet said. "Shall I take you to the changing room and show you your outfits?"

"Yes," said Matt. "We thought you could check out your clothes – in case any of them need to be adjusted. Then you'll start to rehearse your routine with Vicki. OK?"

"Go Glitter!" the girls replied.

They could hardly believe it – after all the excitement over the last couple of weeks, the Glitter Girls were actually going to make two commercials. The Glitter Girls really were the new Ice Brite smiles!

"These are just great!" said Meg, stroking the five white lurex T-shirts that were hanging on a rail in the changing room.

"Wow!" exclaimed Charly. "Aren't they fantastic?"

The T-shirts had the words ICE BRITE written in glittery blue lettering across the front.

"Hey, look at the trousers!" said Zoe, taking some off the rack.

"They are so cool!" agreed Flo.

"And look at these!" Meg said, grabbing a pair of blue and white trainers and stroking them.

"They've got crystals on them!" said Hannah.

"We're hoping that as you dance the lights will catch on the diamonds and make everything sparkle even more," explained Scarlet.

"Fantastic," said Flo.

"Come on – let's see if they fit," Scarlet smiled. "Then we'd better get you back to Vicki so that you can start rehearsing."

"OK, I thought we'd start by listening to the

music," Vicki explained when the Glitter Girls got to the rehearsal studio. "We're using the same musical theme which is going to become immediately recognizable to everyone as the new Ice Brite tune. And there's a dance routine that goes with it."

The Glitter Girls listened as Vicky played a catchy jingle.

"That's really good," said Hannah, tapping her foot to the beat as she listened. The others agreed with her.

"It is, isn't it?" Vicki said smiling. "Come on then – it's a simple routine to learn. I'll do it on my own first so you can see it."

Vicki stepped up to the mirror and began to dance.

"What do you think?" Vicki asked when she'd finished.

"I've done some of those steps in my Modern class," said Hannah.

"It looks hard," confessed Meg.

"But you can learn them!" encouraged Hannah. "Look."

She took her friends by the hand and showed them the opening step that Vicki had done, only more slowly.

"That's it!" said Vicki, sounding pleased. "Now let's all do it up to speed."

The Glitter Girls turned to the front of the studio and copied Vicki. After some mistakes and miscounts, the Glitter Girls began to master the routine. It started with them all tapping their toes to the beat and clicking their fingers. Then they jumped and twirled to the music before jumping once more into the air and waving their arms as they sang, "Ice Brite Glitter! For the smile that's right! The smile that's Ice Brite!" Vicki seemed pleased that they'd managed to pick up the routine quite quickly. She watched them do the routine on their own.

"Right," she said, when they had finished. "Now

you know the steps, I want to see some life in it!"

"What do you mean?" Hannah asked.

"Some smiling!" Vicki said, making an exaggerated smile herself and pointing at her smile with her fingers. "Start to have fun!"

The Glitter Girls laughed and relaxed a bit. Vicki was right – they were concentrating so hard they had all forgotten that one of the reasons why they'd been chosen was because of their smiles!

"Matt's going to fill the set with snow for this commercial," Vicki explained.

"Brilliant!" said Hannah.

"What, *real* snow?" Zoe asked in amazement.

"No," Vicki said. "But it's a really clever fake snow that will have most people fooled. I want you all to have a go at kicking the snow with your feet as you dance but you'll just have to imagine it's there for the time being – do you think you can do that?"

The Glitter Girls had a go – it was difficult but

Vicki said that it would be easier when they got on set.

"Can we do it with the music again?" Meg asked.

Vicki switched it on and danced with them to show them what she meant.

So the Glitter Girls practised even harder until eventually Vicki said they could take a break.

"Matt's going to come in soon and watch how we are getting on."

"When do we start filming?" Meg asked.

"Tomorrow," Vicki said. "We learn the routines today and then shoot the ads tomorrow."

"Wow," said Hannah, feeling slightly worried.

"Do you think we can do it?" Zoe said.

"I don't know," Charly said, biting her bottom lip.

"Come on," said Meg, determinedly. "Of course we can!"

"Go Glitter!" her friends resolved.

Chapter 8

"One, two, three, four!" Vicki counted the Glitter Girls in to the beat of the music. It was a really catchy tune and everyone who had come in to watch them couldn't help but tap their feet to the beat.

Dr Baker and Mr Eng had come in and were sitting on some seats in the front corner. Matt, Vicki and Scarlet were standing in a row with their backs against the mirror. Every now and then they whispered something to each other and pointed at the Glitter Girls.

As the Glitter Girls danced and tried their best to smile as brightly as they could, they wondered what they were saying.

Everything seemed to be going OK until the

very end, when the Glitter Girls tossed their pretend snow into the air and then tried to say their jingle. But they were all breathless and everyone talked at the wrong time so that they spoke over each other. Vicki didn't look very pleased and Matt wasn't at all impressed either.

"That was a disaster!" said Meg.

"Can we try again?" Hannah begged.

"Yes – we managed it at the rehearsal!" pleaded Zoe and Flo.

"Can we try it once more?" Charly asked.

"OK." Matt smiled.

So they had another go. This time, they managed to get the words out OK. But it was still hard to get the timing right before smiling in time for the last note of the tune.

"Much better!" said Matt, after their final time. "Do you reckon you could keep practising that for me?"

"We'll get it right!" Meg said.

"Promise!" the others confirmed.

"Come on then, girls," Vicki said. "Let's rehearse some more."

The Glitter Girls worked with Vicki for the rest of the afternoon. They got more confident with each run-through. And even though they were tired, they loved every minute of it. Eventually, Vicki called the rehearsal to a stop.

"OK – I think it's time you went back to the hotel and chilled out, girls," Vicki said, smiling at them. "You've done really well today and I'm really pleased with you."

"Thanks, Vicki," Charly said.

"It's a pleasure," Vicki said. "Think you'll come back tomorrow then?"

"Go Glitter!" the Glitter Girls confirmed.

When they got back to their hotel that evening, the Glitter Girls didn't think they had ever been so tired in their lives. They had worked really hard at getting everything just perfect. There was so much to think about! Getting the steps right, doing it to the music and saying the words on time, as well as remembering to smile and enjoy it!

"Why don't you girls all have a relaxing bath after your hard work?" Dr Baker suggested, when they were in their suite.

"Bags I go first!" Charly said, desperate to have the chance to relax in the film star-style bath.

"But I'm starving!" said Zoe. "Can't we eat first?"

"Tell you what," Mr Eng said. "Why don't you choose some food from the menu and then you can have it in your room?"

"Can we have a feast?" Flo begged.

"With lots of different food?" Charly pleaded.

"Hmm." Dr Baker looked at Mr Eng and then back at the girls. "Well, I expect you're all pretty hungry after all your hard work today. . . Why not?"

"Yes!" said Hannah, triumphantly.

"But don't go wild and order too much!" Mr Eng laughed.

"Go Glitter!" the Glitter Girls cried, grabbing the menu from next to the phone and starting to choose.

Charly told Meg what she wanted to order and then went off to the bathroom to run her bath. The Glitter Girls had a great time choosing between pizzas, burgers, omelettes, fantastic sandwich fillings – and so many ice creams and puddings! They took ages to make their decisions and then they had to wait impatiently for the food to arrive.

"Hey – this telly's got forty channels!" said Zoe, fiddling with the remote control.

"Is there a cartoon channel?" Charly asked, wandering into the room wearing a sumptuous bathrobe she had found in the wardrobe, which was miles too big for her.

"Let's see," said Flo.

The girls flicked through all the channels trying to decide whether to watch MTV or Nickelodeon. They finally decided on MTV – Gareth Gates's new video was on! They watched that and even had a bit of energy left to sing along.

"You had a quick bath," Hannah said to Charly, who was slumped on the bed next to her.

"Oh, I haven't had it yet!" Charly explained.

"So who's running the bath now?" Meg asked, listening to the sound of running water.

All five of the Glitter Girls were sitting on their beds.

"Oh no!" Charly exclaimed, leaping up and rushing to the bathroom – just in time to meet a sea of bubbles slowly making its way to the door!

"Charly!" Meg yelled as she peered round the bathroom doorway. "There are bubbles everywhere!"

"I think it's going to flood!" said Hannah, rushing in to turn off the taps.

"Oh no!" said Flo. "Here comes my dad – now we're for it!"

Mr Eng pushed his way through the bubbles. "What on earth have you girls done?" He looked pretty cross.

"Nothing, Dad – honestly," Flo said. "We don't know what happened. Charly didn't put that much bubble bath in. . ."

Mr Eng turned off the taps and pulled the plug.

"Oh – I see," he said, his head emerging back up out of the bubbles again. "You twit, Charly! You pushed the jacuzzi button down! No wonder you had so many bubbles."

"Sorry!" Charly said, giggling.

"What are we going to do about all the bubbles though?" Meg wondered.

Just then there was a knock at the door.

"I expect that's room service – with your

feast, no doubt," Dr Baker said. "Time to eat, girls. Then let's see if they can help us to clear this mess up!"

Chapter 9

The Glitter Girls were up bright and early the next morning and were whisked off to the studio in their chauffeur-driven limousine. They couldn't wait for the filming to start.

When the car pulled up outside the studio, the girls bundled out and followed Dr Baker and Mr Eng into the reception area.

"Hello again, girls!" the receptionist said. "Vicki asked if you could go straight into the changing room, please."

Scarlet was in the changing room already.

"OK, girls?" she said. "Can you all get changed into your outfits and then put these big capes on?"

Scarlet pointed to some big plastic capes.

"This is Zac – he's going to do your make-up and hair. The capes will protect your clothes while he does it."

"Hi, girls!" Zac said.

"Hi!" the five best friends grinned.

"Who's first?" Zac asked.

"Me!" they all said at once.

The Glitter Girls' make-up was great! When Zac had finished with them they seemed to shimmer from head to foot. They had glittering powder dusted over their faces and lip gloss that sparkled as well. He even sprayed glitter on their hair!

"Wow!" said Zoe as she stepped out of the changing room and into the studio.

"This is just magic!" Flo exclaimed.

"Can we touch the snow?" Meg asked.

"Sure – go ahead!" Matt said. "In fact, have a practise dancing in it before we start filming."

"You bet!" said Charly rushing over to the set first. It was filled with amazingly bright lights and had a shimmering blue backdrop and floor that was mostly covered in snow.

"Come on – let's have a rehearsal," said Vicki.

The Glitter Girls went through their paces. It was such fun dancing in the snow – and it wasn't at all difficult to imagine it was real snow, in spite of the lights.

"Matt's just going through your positions and the lighting angles," Scarlet explained. "We'll start filming soon."

"It's so hot in here!" said Meg.

"Afraid so," said Matt, coming over to them. "It's the lights. How are you feeling though, girls? We'll do a quick run-through. I want to make sure the camera operators understand what you do and where you are so don't worry if it's not perfect first time round. Ready for action?"

"You bet!" said Charly.

The Glitter Girls were so excited they couldn't wait to start.

"Well, let's not waste any time," Matt said. "OK, everyone?" he called loudly around the studio.

It was a slow start because every time the Glitter Girls got into the swing of the routine, Matt seemed to shout "Cut!" and everything had to stop. There were moments when the girls got too close to the front of the set and Scarlet had to put some masking tape on the floor to show them where they should stop. It seemed like they never got a chance to do the routine the whole way through without being stopped. Matt and the camera operators kept checking things on a machine that played back the filming so far.

"Come and have a look at this, girls," Matt said at one point. "What do you think?"

They watched themselves on the small screen – it was weird in a way, but very cool.

"I think you could do that move there a bit better, don't you?" Vicki said, re-running one section. "Let's have a quick try without the cameras rolling."

The Glitter Girls went through their paces and then Matt said, "OK, everyone – lights, camera, action!"

The Glitter Girls spun and leapt across the set, trying to imagine that they really were playing in the snow in the cold rather than feeling very warm with the electric lights on them!

"It's a wrap!" said Matt. "That was much better! We might just try one more take after lunch but let's stop for a break."

The Glitter Girls were more than happy to change out of their Ice Brite clothes and have something to eat. Everyone on the set ate together.

"Matt?" Meg asked when she'd finished her first sandwich. "When will the commercials be on television?"

"I'm not exactly sure," Matt explained. "But it will be a few months before you see them probably."

"Oh. . ." Zoe was as disappointed as her friends. They had hoped that they would see themselves on TV really soon.

"Don't worry," Scarlet said, realizing how they felt. "We'll show you the rushes of the ads before you go today."

"The rushes?" Charly asked. "What are they?"

"That's a rough version of the ads before they are edited and the sound is dubbed properly."

"Cool!" smiled Hannah. "I can't wait."

★ ♥ ★ ♥ ★ ♥ ★

After changing back into their Ice Brite outfits, Zac made sure the girls hair was OK before the Glitter Girls were back in action. Just as before lunch, it seemed that every time they stopped filming, Zac leapt on to the set to brush on some more powder or to pat a stray hair in place.

"OK," said Matt. "Just one more go and I think we're done. Everyone in position, please!"

It was the Glitter Girls' last chance to look fantastic. They put every ounce of energy they had left into making their routine as great as they could.

"The smile that's right – the smile that's Ice Brite!" the Glitter Girls grinned.

The final note of the jingle faded.

"Cut!"

The studio was silent. Had the Glitter Girls been OK? They looked expectantly at each other and then at Matt and Vicki. But before anyone could say anything more, the whole studio broke into applause.

"That was perfect, girls," Matt said, coming over to them.

"It was fab! You were great," agreed Vicki.

"I wish everyone I worked with was as professional as you lot," said Matt, laughing.

The Glitter Girls looked at each other and grinned.

"Have you had as good a time as we have?" asked Vicki.

"You bet!" the Glitter Girls all said at once.

Vicki smiled. "I think it's time you went back to the hotel and got some rest before tomorrow's photoshoot."

"Go Glitter!" the girls agreed.

Chapter 10

When the Glitter Girls had first heard that they would be staying in a hotel for two nights, they imagined that they would stay up late partying. But in reality, the Glitter Girls were just too tired after working so hard at the studio each day!

In fact, on the Friday morning, Dr Baker and Mr Eng had a hard job waking them.

"Come on, you lot!" Flo's dad yelled. "If you don't get up soon you won't have time for breakfast!"

Eventually, the Glitter Girls were ready and they even managed to arrive at the studio on time.

"Hi girls!" said Scarlet, as she met them in

reception. "Come and meet Cherry – she's our photographer."

The Glitter Girls followed Scarlet into the studio they had worked in for the last two days. There was the snow scene from the day before, but instead of camera operators this time there was just a tripod with a camera on the top.

A tall girl with long blonde hair and a boy with dark hair were arranging some lights. They looked up as the Glitter Girls came in.

"Hello, I'm Cherry and you must be the Glitter Girls," the girl said, walking over to greet them. "I'm going to be taking your photos and this is my assistant, Tony, who helps with the lighting and things."

"Hi girls," Tony said.

"Hello," said the Glitter Girls.

"Who's who?" Cherry asked, and the Glitter Girls introduced themselves.

"So, what's going to happen today?" Meg asked.

"Well, I'll be taking some still photographs of you all for the ad campaign. I've been looking through the work you shot yesterday," Cherry explained. "It's looking really great – you're naturals in front of the camera."

"Thanks," said Charly.

"Right," said Cherry. "We should probably get going because I gather you girls have to get off home this afternoon."

"Yes," said Hannah sadly. Like her friends, she wanted this adventure to go on and on – it was so much fun.

"Morning, everyone!" said Zac, walking into the studio. "Let's get Ice Brite Glittery!"

Half an hour later, the Glitter Girls were having a great time.

"Imagine you are having a party!" Cherry encouraged them. "Smile!"

Tony kept telling them really cheesy jokes and the Glitter Girls were laughing and having lots of fun.

"Can we tell you some jokes?" Meg asked.

"Yes," said Zoe. "I reckon our jokes are better than yours!"

And so the morning passed with Cherry clicking away with her camera and Tony and the Glitter Girls seeing who could make everyone laugh the most.

"This all seems to be going well," said Matt, coming into the studio for the first time that day.

"Hi Matt!" the girls said.

"You've come in just at the right time," Cherry explained. "The girls are going to take a break before we start the last shots."

"Time for lunch then, girls?" Scarlet said, coming into the studio.

"You bet," they agreed.

★ ♥ ★ ♥ ★ ♥ ★

The afternoon whizzed by with the Glitter Girls back on set.

"You girls act like you've been modelling all your lives!" Cherry said, as she snapped away with her camera.

"Go Glitter!" the girls replied, raising their arms in the air in agreement.

"Good shot!" said Cherry, capturing the moment for ever.

At the end of the afternoon, Matt and Cherry told the girls how pleased they were with everything.

"Here," said Cherry, handing each of the Glitter Girls a set of Polaroid shots she had taken throughout the shoot to check that the lighting was right. "These will give you an idea of the final thing."

"And they're a great souvenir to take home with us," Meg said.

"Yes," agreed her friends.

"Will the ads be in magazines?" Flo asked.

"Yes," said Matt. "And maybe some other things, like bus stops and billboards."

"Go Glitter!" cried the Glitter Girls excitedly – they were going to see their faces everywhere!

Chapter 11

Back home, life seemed a bit dull for the Glitter Girls after all the excitement in Birmingham. Weeks went by and the Glitter Girls kept a keen eye on the television, hoping to see their advertisements. But as Dr Baker reminded them, Matt had said it would be a few months before anything was going to be on TV.

"I reckon you made it all up," Jack, Meg's brother, said one day when the five best friends were all having tea at Meg's house.

"Did not!" said Meg, pulling a face at her brother.

"Well, when are these commercials going to be on telly then?" Jack said triumphantly. "Never – that's when."

"So if we made it all up," said Charly, "how come we got paid some money?"

"And where did we get our Ice Brite T-shirts and jeans from if we didn't make the commercials?" said Zoe.

"Huh!" said Jack. There wasn't much else he could say because it was true. Mrs Morgan laughed as she put down another plate of sandwiches on the table.

"Actually, that reminds me," she said. "There's been a letter for you today, Meg. Here!" She handed an official-looking envelope to Meg.

"Who's it from?" Hannah asked, leaning over her friend's shoulder as she opened the letter.

"Wow!" Meg exclaimed. "We've got invitations to attend *Cinderella on Ice*!"

"What?" wondered Zoe. "Why?"

Meg looked down at the letter again and explained further. "Ice Brite are sponsoring the show. . . And they are launching the new glittery toothpaste and the commercials on the first night! . . .They want us to go and present a bouquet to the star of the show!"

"You mean we've got to skate?" Hannah asked, looking a bit concerned. "I'm not good at skating!"

"When?" Charly asked.

"Um . . . next month," Meg said. "And Ice Brite have arranged for us to have skating lessons before!"

The five best friends couldn't believe their luck!

"It's a fix!" moaned Jack.

"You're just jealous!" said Meg.

And the Glitter Girls laughed.

★ ♥ ★ ♥ ★ ♥ ★

The Glitter Girls had skating lessons every weekend after that. They all knew how to skate, just not that well! Cara, their skating teacher, had been asked to teach them how to skate across the rink, stop and then present a bouquet. The first time they tried, it was a disaster because the girls simply couldn't stop! But by their last lessons they had managed to perfect it – in time to go to London for the premiere of *Cinderella on Ice*.

The Glitter Girls travelled by train to London with their parents. They were met at the station by Sonya, the publicity girl from Ice Brite.

"It's so great to meet you all at last," she said. "Everyone is so looking forward to tonight. The director of the company will be there too. He is so pleased with your advertisements. Come on – there's a special minibus outside to take us to the rink."

It was dark as the Glitter Girls set off in the bus but they looked around excitedly as they made the journey across London. It was a slow journey because there was so much traffic and they kept having to stop.

"Hey, look!" Charly shouted.

"What?" asked Flo.

"Over there!" Charly pointed. "It's us!"

And it was! It was one of Cherry's photographs. The Glitter Girls were smiling out from the side of a bus!

"It's great, isn't it?" said Sonya. "The campaign starts this evening. We're having a launch party for the new Ice Brite toothpaste tonight – you'll definitely see the finished ads there. And you'll be all over the place by tomorrow morning."

"Go Glitter!" the five best friends gulped.

★ ♥ ★ ♥ ★ ♥ ★

When they reached the ice rink, Sonya took them behind the scenes to meet some others from the company.

"We are just delighted with the Ice Brite campaign," the Managing Director of Ice Brite told the Glitter Girls. "If it goes well, we may even need you to do some more ads for us."

The Glitter Girls exchanged excited glances.

"What do we have to do now?" Charly asked Sonya, after the Managing Director had left for an important meeting before the evening's launch.

"Well, I know you've all learnt how to present the bouquet," Sonya said. "But we've got some great Ice Brite skating outfits for you, with special skates too. Why don't I take you to change while your parents take their seats in the box?"

"Yes, please!" said Flo, and the Glitter Girls were soon following Sonya to a changing room especially for them.

They couldn't believe their eyes when they saw the gorgeous silvery-white dresses and matching little capes trimmed with snowy feathers.

"Hey, look at these skates!" said Charly, delicately stroking the boots that shimmered with sparkly jewels in the light.

"And look at the lovely bouquet!" exclaimed Hannah.

"Wow!" sighed Meg and Zoe.

"Now, how would you like to meet the cast for a quick practice before the show starts?" Sonya asked.

"Brilliant!" the Glitter Girls said.

Even though they were nervous about making their skating debut in front of so many people, the Glitter Girls were made to feel welcome by all of the cast.

"We've heard all about you," said the girl who played Cinderella. "We've seen the ads too – you look great!"

"Thanks," called the girls as she skated off to take up her position.

"Come on," said the boy who played Prince Charming. "Let's see if the six of us can skate over to Cinderella without falling over!"

They ran through the finale and then the Glitter Girls rehearsed their bit. After all their practising at the rink at home, the Glitter Girls' skating went quite well.

"Phew," said Flo. "I was getting worried about making a fool of myself!"

"It'll be fine," Sonya reassured them. "Come on – let's take you to your special rink-side seats before the show starts!"

A few minutes later, the Glitter Girls were back with their parents and settled into a special box right at the front of the rink, which gave them easy acccess to the ice.

"Isn't this fantastic?" said Hannah when the introductory music started up.

"Brilliant!" agreed Charly.

The whole show was totally spectacular. The skaters were brilliant and they whizzed across the rink so fast it sometimes seemed that they didn't even touch the ice with their feet. There were songs that the whole audience joined in with and the costumes were amazing – especially Cinderella's ballgown, which sparkled brilliantly under the lights.

"Come on," Sonya whispered, just as the finale music started up. "It's your turn! Time to get your boots on!"

The Glitter Girls slipped out of their seats and put on their boots before they stepped down to the edge of the rink. They watched as every skater linked up and they skated fast in a long line all around the rink.

"Are you girls ready?" said Prince Charming, skimming to a stop next to them.

"Yes," they all replied at once, feeling nervous at having to skate in front of such a huge crowd of people.

As the music ended, a voice announced to the audience. "And now, please welcome the Glitter Girls! The girls with the smile that's right – the smile that's Ice Brite!"

Prince Charming led the Glitter Girls across

the ice before they came to a perfect stop in front of Cinderella. The Glitter Girls had decided that Charly should present Cinderella with her sparkly bouquet and, as she did so there was a great flash of lights as photographers took pictures!

"Isn't this amazing!" said Meg, looking around the ice rink at the hundreds of people who were clapping and cheering.

"Fantastic," agreed Hannah, beaming.

"Come on, girls," Cinderella said. "Let's take a final bow before we whisk you off to the party."

"Go Glitter!" the five best friends cheered and bowed gracefully to the audience.

"You were great, girls!" said Mr Gordon when the Glitter Girls' parents met up with them at the party.

"Thanks." The girls grinned with pleasure and excitement.

"It was such fun," said Charly. "And none of us fell over!"

The party was being held in a big room that had been specially decorated. There was more fake snow, ice sculptures and yummy food and drink everywhere. The ceiling was hung with silver streamers and balloons. And on the walls were posters of the photographs that Cherry had taken.

"This is amazing," said Flo.

"And look at the posters!" Hannah said.

"They're all across the country!" Sonya grinned.

"And so are the Glitter Girls!" Zoe laughed.

"We're really proud of you," said Mrs Gordon.

"Yes – it's great that you were chosen out of all those other girls," said Mrs Morgan, hugging Meg. "But I hope you're ready for fame!"

"I can hear your phone beeping, Mum," said Meg.

"Oh yes!" said Mrs Morgan, releasing Meg and pulling her phone from her bag. "It's a message – from Jack!"

The Glitter Girls pretended to groan and giggled.

"What does he want?" Meg wondered.

"Probably to see if we really did go to the ice show!" Charly laughed.

"So what *does* he say?" asked Hannah.

"Here." Mrs Morgan smiled and handed the phone over to the girls. They all peered at the text message which read: JUST SEEN G GIRLS ON TV!

"The television commercials must have started too!" said Meg.

"Now Jack'll have to eat his words!" giggled Flo.

"Go Glitter!" her friends laughed.

Out now:

Magazine Mania

There was another meeting of the magazine contributors on Thursday after school.

"Look at this!" said Miss Stanley, holding up the front page of the newspaper that had come out that morning.

WOW! CALLING ALL OLD WELLS ROAD PUPILS! read the headline of the article at the bottom of the front page. Beside it, there was a great picture of all the boys and girls holding their arms out and saying, "Wow!"

"That's fab!" said Meg.

Miss Stanley read some of the article aloud to everyone: " '*The school's young editorial team are looking for former pupils. So, however long ago you left, please write in to tell them what you are doing now and if you have any special memories – including photos – of your time at Wells Road.*' That should stir lots of memories!" Miss Stanley said. "And I love the photo!"

"What are we going to do now though?" Meg asked.

"Well – I need to find out who's already started on their section of the magazine," Miss Stanley said. "Also, I want to give you all this timetable I've worked out." She handed everyone a sheet of paper and they all started to read it.

"Any questions?" Miss Stanley asked.

"When can I start putting everything together on the computer?" Flo wanted to know.

"As soon as possible," their teacher replied. "But we need to find out if everyone thinks they can stick to this timetable first. Amy, you go first – how are you getting on?"

★ ♥ ★ ♥ ★ ♥ ★

The Glitter Girls met up in Meg's house after school that day. They were having a great time braiding each other's hair and making friendship bracelets.

"So who are you going to interview for the magazine, Charly?" Flo asked.

"I don't know," Charly said as she started to weave a tassel of silver charms through Zoe's hair.

"Well, you'll have to think of someone soon," said Meg.

"I know!" Charly sighed. "But the only person I can think of at the moment is Mrs Wadhurst and, well, I don't want to be rude, but she's not that exciting, is she?"

"I know what you mean," agreed Hannah. "You really need someone who people don't know much about."

"Difficult one," said Zoe. "But you're bound to think of someone."

"Maybe there's someone who's coming to do a play at the theatre where Hannah's mum works?" Meg suggested.

"I could ask my mum," said Hannah.

"That's a brilliant idea," agreed Charly. "Please can you ask her tonight?"

"Yes, sure," Hannah said, smiling at her friend.

"I wish we could write a feature on hair and make-up," said Flo, admiring Zoe's hair.

"But Amy's doing the fashion column. . ." Hannah confirmed.

"Yes – but she's not going to write about hair braids, is she?" said Charly. "We could write about how to make different designs with braids and plaits. Maybe even some body-art stuff."

"Maybe we could persuade Miss Stanley to add another column to the magazine," suggested Flo, eagerly. "I'd have to change that plan I made."

"But even if there is enough space," Meg said, thinking aloud. "How will we know what people want us to write about?"

"We could ask them to tell us!" said Hannah.

"That's it!" said Meg, suddenly stopping the plait she was doing in Hannah's hair and finishing it off with a sparkly purple hair tie. She pulled her notebook out. "We could ask other girls in school if they have any questions – you know, about how to do braids and special make-up effects."

"Then we could answer them!" grinned Charly.

"And we could call it 'Go Glitter'!" suggested Flo.

"Go Glitter!" all her friends agreed.

Don't miss:

Summer Special

Hurray for the summer holidays! And this summer's extra-special because the Glitter Girls get to go away with ALL their friends!

The girls are super-excited about all the fun activities at summer camp. But a disaster at the beach one day threatens to ruin their trip – can the Glitter Girls save the day and make their holiday the best ever. . .?!